The Senses
SMELL

Angela Royston

Chrysalis Education

Distributed in the United States by
Smart Apple Media
2140 Howard Drive West
North Mankato, Minnesota 56003

Library of Congress Control Number: 2004108660

ISBN 1-59389-201-2

Editorial Manager: Joyce Bentley
Senior Editor: Rasha Elsaeed
Editorial Assistant: Camilla Lloyd

Produced by Bender Richardson White, U.K.
Project Editor: Lionel Bender
Designer: Ben White
Production: Kim Richardson
Picture Researcher: Cathy Stastny
Cover Make-up: Mike Pilley, Radius

Printed in China

10 9 8 7 6 5 4 3 2 1

Words in **bold** can be found in New words on page 31.

Picture credits
Cover: Bubbles/Loisjoy Thurstun.
Inside: Bubbles: pages 4 (Lucy Tizard), 6 (Sarah Vivian Prescot), 9 (Loisjoy Thurstun), 10 (Loisjoy Thurstun), 11 (David Robinson), 13 (Claire Paxton), 14 (Loisjoy Thurstun), 17 (Chris Rout), 19 (Loisjoy Thurstun), 20 (Ian West), 23 (Frans Rombout), 24 (Frans Rombout), 25 (Ian West), 27 (Ian West), 28 (Angela Hampton), 29 (Loisjoy Thurstun). Corbis Images Inc.: pages 15 (Joel Stettenheim), 21 (Corbis Royalty-free), 26 (Nick Hawkes/Ecoscene). Steve Gorton: pages 1, 2, 5, 7, 8. 12, 16, 18, 22.

Contents

What is smell?

Smell is the **sense** that tells you about **scents**, **odors**, and **fumes** in the air around you.

Your nose and brain work together to give you your sense of smell.

Into your nose

When you breathe in, air goes through your **nostrils**.

Inside your nose are many tiny **nerve endings**. These detect smells in the air.

Floating in air

Something smells when **particles** of it float in the air that you breathe.

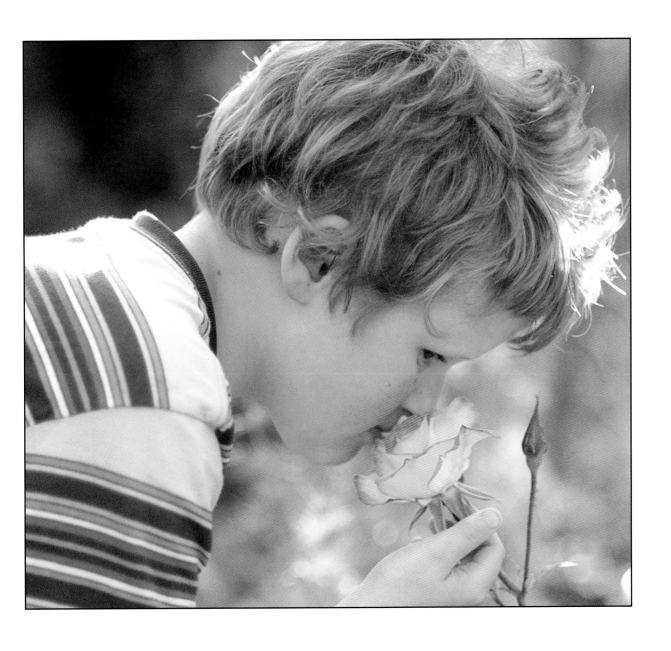

You smell a flower when
some of its particles go into
your nose.

Sweet smells

Perfume smells sweet. Most people like sweet smells.

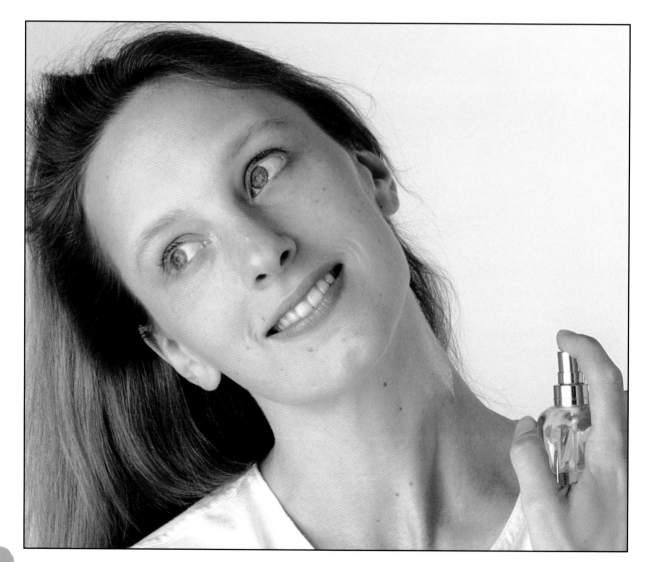

In a food market, the sweet smells of fruit fill the air.

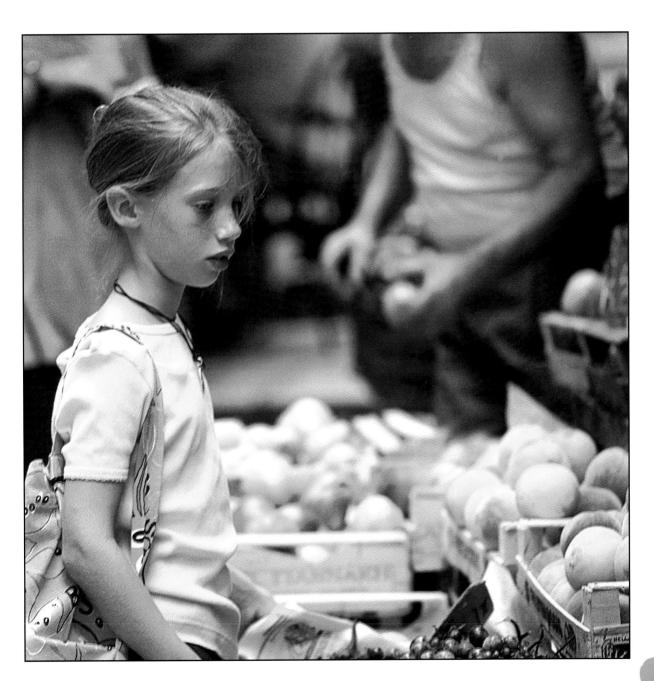

Fresh smells

Green leaves and grasses smell fresh and clean.

Mint smells very fresh, too.
Most toothpastes smell of mint.

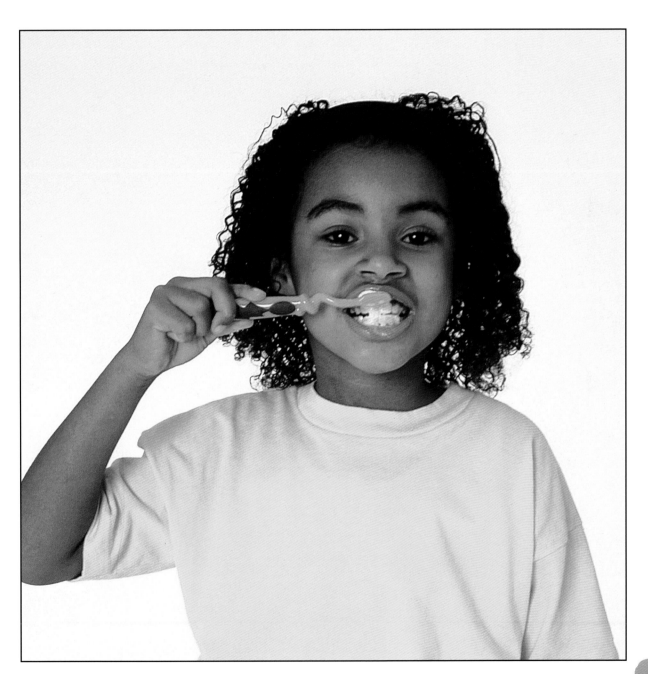

Strong smells

Strong smells are easy to **recognize**. Cut up onions and garlic smell very strong.

Tarmacadam, the black material used to cover roads, also has a strong smell.

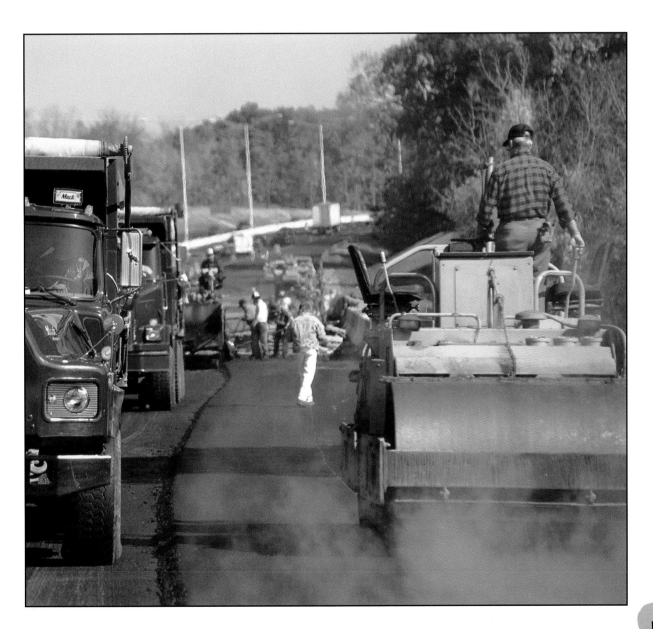

Cooking smells

Cooked food smells such as fried fish, tomato soup, and roast chicken are easy to recognize.

Newly baked cookies smell so good you want to eat them straight away.

Nasty smells

Rotten food smells nasty. This warns you not to eat it.

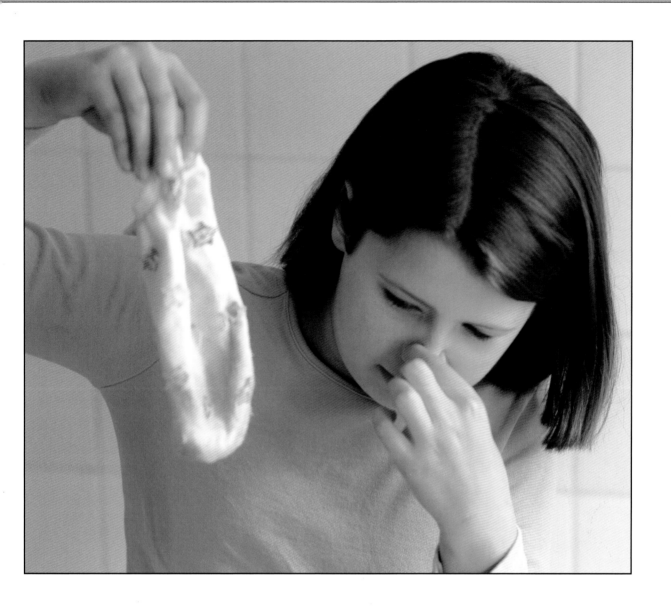

Sweaty socks and shoes can smell really horrible!

Outdoor smells

At the seaside, the smells of seaweed, saltwater, and sand fill the air.

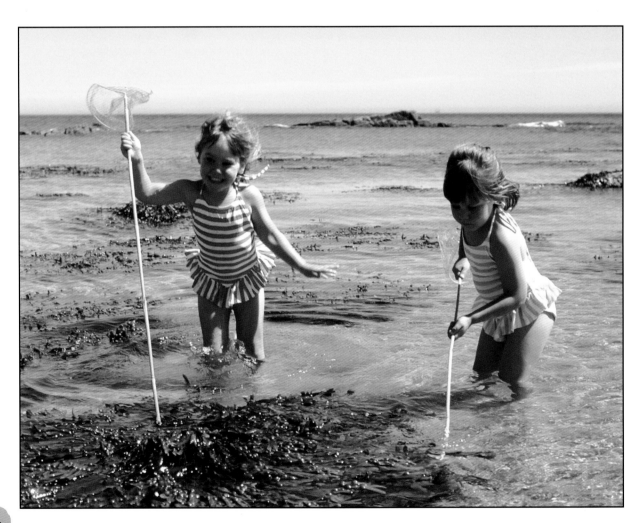

Factory chimneys release smells high in the air. Wind blows the smells far and wide.

Smell and taste

Your senses of smell and taste are similar. These cheeses smell and taste very strong.

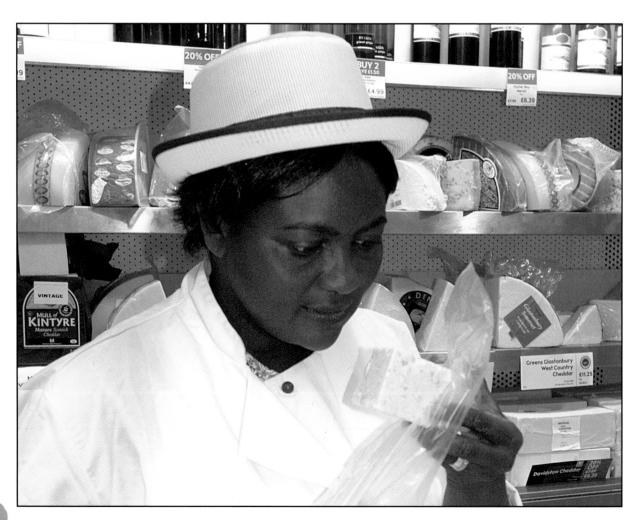

The smell of food cooked on a barbecue can make you feel hungry.

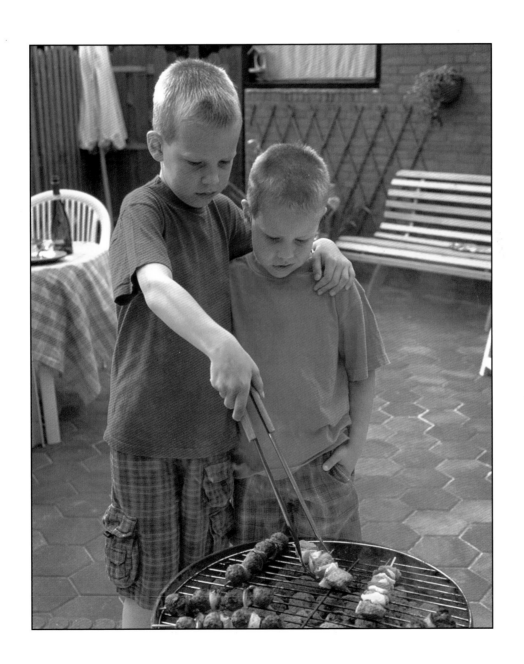

Memories

Babies recognize their mother because they remember how she smells.

The smell of a farm reminds
you of other farms and
zoos you have visited.

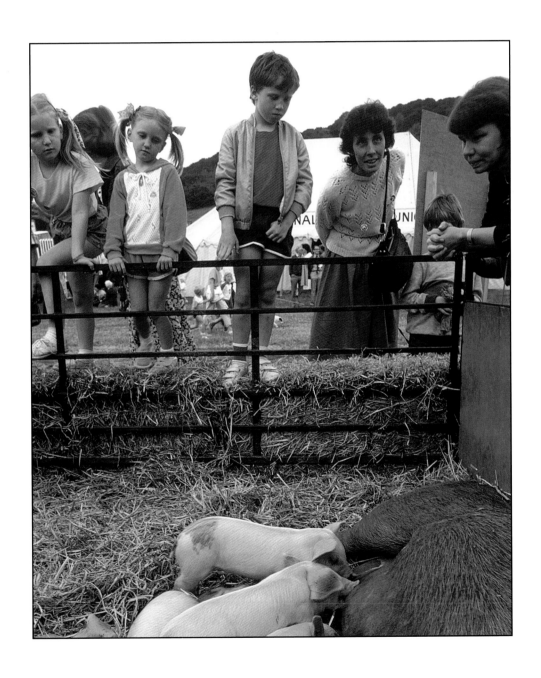

Danger!

The smell of smoke warns you that something is burning.

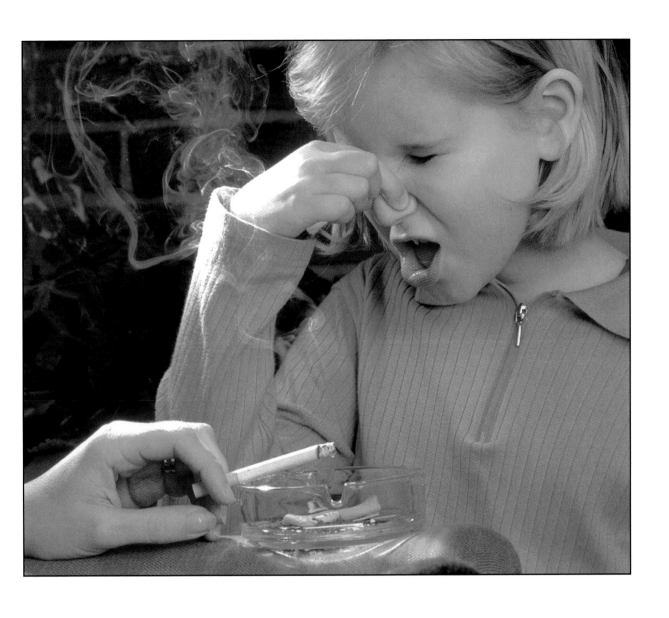

The smell of a cigarette is strong and not very pleasant.

Smelling well

You cannot smell when you have a cold and your nose is blocked. But it will soon clear.

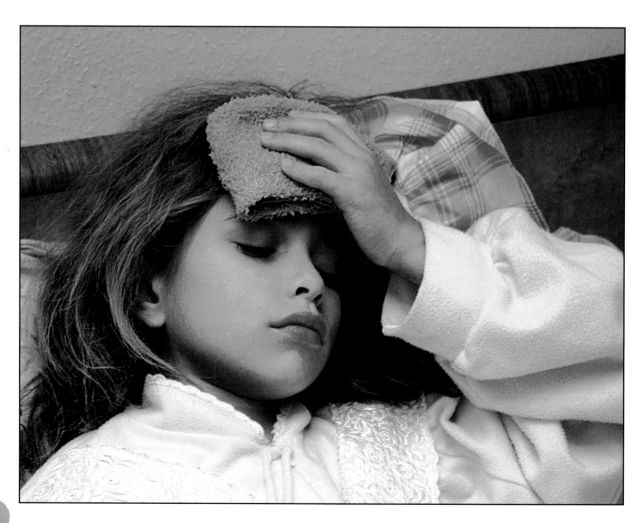

Look after your nose and sense of smell! Blow your nose gently to get rid of **mucus**.

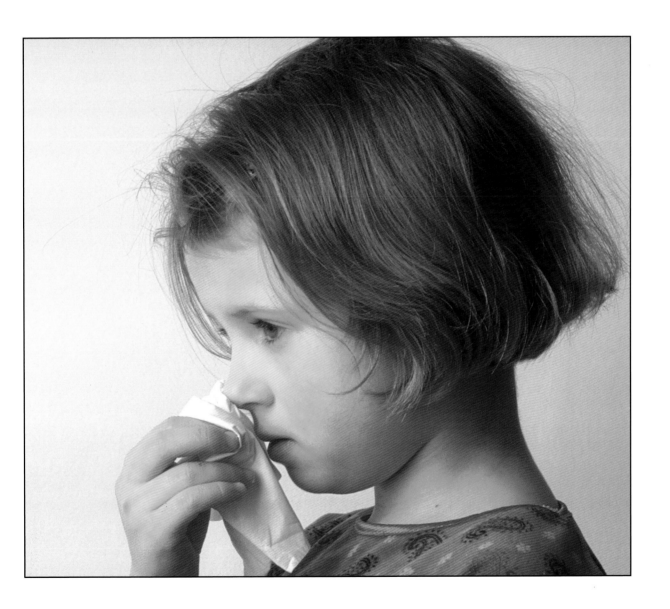

Quiz

1 How does air get inside your nose?

2 What makes something smell?

3 What does perfume smell like?

4 What kind of smell does toothpaste have?

5 Which smells are easiest to recognize?

6 Why does rotten food smell nasty?

7 How does a baby recognize its mother?

8 What happens when you have a cold?

The answers are all in this book!

New words

fumes   smelly pollution in the air, such as car exhausts and factory smoke.

mint   a herb with a strong, fresh taste and smell.

mucus   thick liquid made inside your body.

nerve endings   parts of the body that react to particular things, such as smells.

nostril   opening into your nose.

odor   natural, bad smells, for example sweaty feet, unwashed clothes, and rotten food.

particle   a tiny part of any solid, liquid, or gas that is too small to see.

perfume   something that people put on their skin to make them smell nice.

recognize   know what something is.

scents   natural, pleasant smells such as those from flowers.

sense   the way you find out about your surroundings. You have five senses—sight, hearing, smell, taste, and touch.

sweaty   full of sweat from a person's body.

Index